Josh
9/3/92

The Doggonest
Vacation

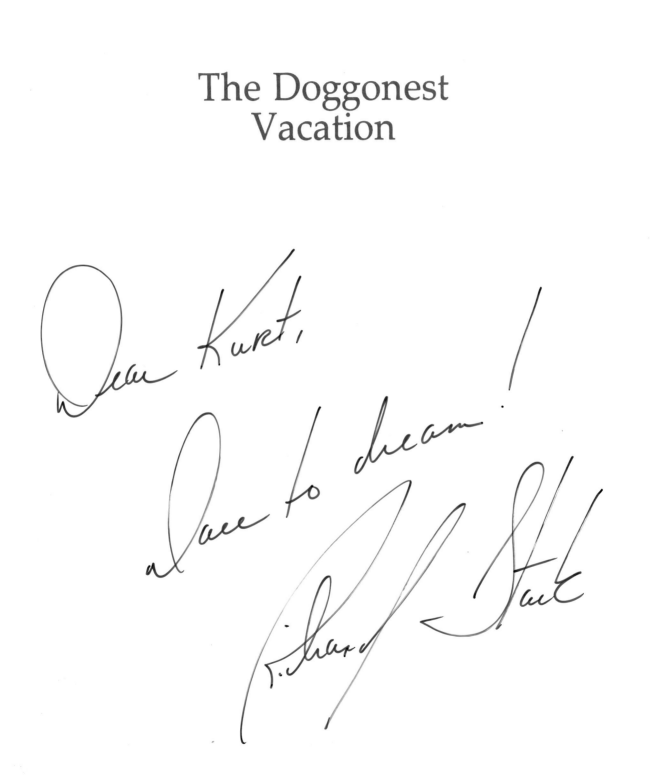

Dear Kurt,

dare to dream!

Richard Stack

The Doggonest Vacation

by

Richard Lynn Stack

Illustrations by Sheri Lynn Mowrer

The Doggonest Vacation

by Richard Lynn Stack

Illustrations by Sheri Lynn Mowrer

Also by Richard Lynn Stack: The Doggonest Christmas

Illustrations by Charles W. Stack

Book produced by Neal Kimmel and Karen Blakeley Camp

Copyright 1990, Richard Lynn Stack

Printed in U.S.A. by Taylor Publishing Company, Dallas, Texas.

Distributed by: Windmill Press, 7609 Beaver Road, Glen Burnie, Maryland, 21061

ISBN 0-9628262-0-0

Library of Congress 90-071706

Dedicated to Anne E. Stack, who helped my dreams come true, by sacrificing her own. Thanks, Mom.

It was springtime in the little town of Bobsled, where Josh lived happily with a kind lady named Miss Elly. Josh thought often of that one very special Christmas when he saved the life of Santa Claus. He had learned to believe in himself, and would never again think of himself as a worthless mutt.

One morning, the postman delivered a letter to Miss Elly, with a postmark that read "Crab Cove, Maryland." Miss Elly was smiling as she opened it and began to read.

"Look Josh," said Miss Elly, "it's from your Uncle Leo, my very dear brother. He writes that he has discovered some doggies in Maryland who need help, and wants to show us what he is doing for them. Would you like to take a vacation?"

"Wow, Oh Bow Wow!" Josh yapped, as he showered Miss Elly with lots of big kisses. "My very first vacation!"

"I'm really excited, too," said Miss Elly. "Maybe I can help Leo with my special dog food."

Miss Elly started packing their suitcases, while Josh ran to tell his friends where he was going. The friends were happy for him, but also just a little bit jealous.

Before long, Josh and Miss Elly were climbing into the taxicab which would take them to Bobsled Airport. The friends were all there to see them off.

"Wow, Oh Bow Wow," yapped Josh, as the taxi started down the street.

"Wow, Oh Bow Wow," echoed the friends, as Brownie and Mackie raced around playfully.

It was a long trip from Bobsled to Crab Cove, but the many wonderful sights along the way made the time go by quickly. As the airplane touched gently down at Friendship Airport, the pilot announced their arrival in Maryland.

Uncle Leo lived in a big white house, nestled by the eastern shore of the Chesapeake Bay. He hurried out to greet them as they made their way down his driveway.

Josh had never met Uncle Leo, but knew right away that he was going to like him. Uncle Leo gave the little dog a warm hug, as Josh showered him with lots of big kisses.

"Josh, did you know that Miss Elly is allergic to dogs?" asked Uncle Leo, as he winked at his silver-haired sister.

"Miss Elly — allergic to dogs?" Josh wondered to himself. The look on his face showed how puzzled he was.

"Sure," laughed Uncle Leo. "You must have noticed that every time she hugs a dog, she breaks out — in a great big smile!"

Josh realized that Uncle Leo had been kidding him. "Wow, Oh Bow Wow," he laughed, as Miss Elly blushed with pride.

When Miss Elly and Josh were settled in, Uncle Leo told them about his discovery of some tired and hungry dogs, living in a nearby forest. These dogs desperately needed homes, and the love of caring people.

Uncle Leo was using part of his home as a shelter, and was letting the dogs live with him. He was determined to find a home for each and every one of them.

"The forest is a fun place to play," reminded Uncle Leo, "but not a nice place for dogs to live."

Later, Uncle Leo introduced them to some of the dogs living in his home. They also met Mr. Henry, who was helping Uncle Leo with his shelter. Mr. Henry was a gentle old man, whose manner was soothing and quiet.

That night, Miss Elly and Josh slept soundly in Uncle Leo's guest bedroom. Josh curled up at the bottom of the bed, his head resting comfortably on Miss Elly's feet.

"Wow, Oh Bow Wow," Josh sighed, as he thought of all that he had seen that day. Then he drifted off to sleep.

The next morning, Josh was awakened by delicious aromas which floated upstairs from the kitchen below. He waited for Miss Elly to open her eyes. He was anxious to play with his new friends, and began tugging at her bed sheets like an impatient child on Christmas morning.

When Miss Elly and Josh came downstairs, they found that Uncle Leo was already making breakfast for them. Uncle Leo knew that his furry guests in the shelter would also be hungry. When Miss Elly offered to cook a big pot of her special dog food, Uncle Leo gladly accepted.

Suddenly, everyone was startled by the sound of growling, vicious and unlike anything Josh had ever heard. He ran to the shelter to see what was happening, with Miss Elly and Uncle Leo following close behind him. What they saw was terrifying, for a big brown dog was snapping and

snarling at Mr. Henry. The old man stood very still, with his leash dangling from his hand. He was unhurt, but looked as though he were afraid to move.

The big dog seemed also to be frightened. His teeth were bared, and the hair on the back of his neck stood up like a stiff hairbrush. His golden eyes flashed a look of anger, as he looked for a way out of the room. A door had been left open behind him, and he bolted through it, racing away from the house. Everyone watched as the big dog disappeared into the woods where Uncle Leo had found him.

Miss Elly knelt down to calm her little dog, who could not stop trembling. Josh wondered why Uncle Leo had allowed such a mean dog into his home. Miss Elly could tell what he was thinking.

"Josh," she cautioned, "we should try not to judge others, especially without knowing anything about them."

"Dogs are like people," agreed Uncle Leo. "When dogs act this way, it usually is because they have been mistreated. The big dog is a Chesapeake Bay Retriever, and we call him 'Trevor'. This type of dog is often used for hunting. We don't know much about him, but we suspect that someone has hurt him badly."

To his surprise, Josh saw that even Mr. Henry did not seem to be angry with Trevor. He began to understand what they were trying to tell him.

It soon became clear that the big dog was not coming back, and someone would have to go look for him. They agreed that Josh would have the best chance of finding Trevor. Miss Elly could tell that he really wanted to try.

"Please be careful," said Miss Elly. "Trevor is scared, and doesn't seem to trust people. He may not trust you, either."

Josh nodded his head, to let Miss Elly know that he understood. Then he raced out the door, and followed Trevor into the forest.

It was almost dark b
fore Josh finally caug
up with the big, brown dog, who w
drinking thirstily from a shallo
stream.

"Hi, Trevor," said Josh, as he walk
cautiously out from behind some tree

Trevor looked up, his eyes watchi
for any sign of danger. "Who are you
he demanded, "and how do you kno
my name?"

Trevor's voice sounded threatenin
and it caused Josh to stop in his tracks.

Nervously, the little dog told Trevor his name. "I'm here on vacation," added Josh, "and I saw what happened this morning. Everyone is worried about you, and would like you to come back with me."

"No," said Trevor. "I'm never going to let people hurt me again. When that man walked into the room with a leash, I just knew he was going to hit me with it."

"Mr. Henry's leash is used for helping dogs," explained Josh, "and never for hitting them." He smiled as he described what a gentle person Mr. Henry was.

"Miss Elly and Uncle Leo love animals, too," he continued. "They just want to be our friends."

The dogs talked for a long time, and Josh was able to gain Trevor's trust. The big dog realized how mistaken he had been about Mr. Henry, and then was ashamed for the way he had behaved.

"My master believes that all Retrievers should be hunting dogs," explained Trevor. "But animals are my friends and I love them. Because I refuse to hunt my friends, he calls me a 'sissy,' and hits me with my leash."

"When I was a puppy and he hit me, I growled a little bit," Trevor said quietly. "The Master put a big muzzle over my face to punish me."

Josh could feel his eyes filling with tears, and he tried to blink them away.

"I love the Master," Trevor continued, "and really wish he liked me. But he treated me so badly that I ran away from home. I didn't know what else to do."

"You're not a sissy," said Josh, "just because you don't want to hunt your friends. Miss Elly and Uncle Leo don't hunt, and many people like and respect them. I'm sure that they can help you, if you will just give them a chance."

Trevor listened carefully to what Josh was telling him, and finally agreed to go back with him. But by now, it was pitch dark, and the dogs were miles from Uncle Leo's house. They decided to stay there for the night, and begin their long walk back in the morning.

Josh and Trevor bedded down under a big tree, snuggling close to keep each other warm, but also for a little extra courage. Trevor listened as Josh said his prayers, and started to cry when the little dog asked forgiveness for the Master.

Josh and Trevor were "dog-tired," and at first light, they were still fast asleep. When Josh finally awoke, he could not feel Trevor's warm body next to him anymore. Suddenly, there was the sound of shouting, and he realized that something was very wrong.

Josh opened his eyes, and saw an angry-looking man standing over him. The man had a long gun in one hand, and was holding onto Trevor with the other.

Josh knew right away that the man was Trevor's master.

"Now I have you again," yelled the Master.
"I am going to make a hunting dog out of you
— or else."

Trevor struggled with all his might, but the

Master was too strong for him. The Master had decided what he wanted Trevor to become, and his mind would let him think of nothing else.

So during his struggle with Trevor, the Master did not notice when his gun became dangerously clogged with dirt.

Josh watched helplessly as the Master dragged Trevor down to the Bay, toward a boat tied at the water's edge. The little dog could feel his heart breaking as the Master pulled Trevor into the boat, and pushed off from shore.

Trevor looked back at Josh. His golden eyes were now filled with sadness.

"I'll get help," shouted Josh, and he began running as fast as his little legs would carry him. But Uncle Leo's house was far away, and help would be a long time coming.

When the boat reached the deepest part of the bay, the Master stopped rowing. His eyes searched the sky intently, looking for something to shoot.

Trevor watched as the Master shouldered his gun, and aimed it at some majestic ducks which flew high overhead. The big dog had a sick feeling in his stomach. He knew that the Master was going to shoot one of his friends, and he did not want to watch. The big dog closed his eyes — and waited.

Trevor had heard the Master shoot his gun many times before, but this time the noise was louder and different. It was followed by a cry of pain, and the sound of a loud splash. Trevor opened his eyes to see the Master, thrashing around in the choppy water.

The dirt in the Master's gun had caused it to blow up, and the gun lay shattered in the bottom of the boat. The Master's eyes were badly hurt, and he had fallen overboard.

"Help me Trevor!," yelled the Master. "I can't see!"
Waves were hitting against the boat, which made it
hard for Trevor to keep his balance. One minute he
would see the Master bobbing up and down like a
cork. Then the Master would disappear behind
a wall of water.

Trevor knew that unless he acted quickly, the Master would probably drown.
He leaped out of the boat and fought
his way over to the Master. The big
dog looked back, and saw that
the wind and waves were
pushing the boat far away
from them. Soon, Trevor
could not see it any-
more.

Without his eyesight, the Master splashed around helplessly in the water. Finally, his hands found Trevor's collar, and clutched it tightly.

"Please save me," begged the Master, as he hung on in desperation.

Immediately, Trevor began swimming toward the far-away shore, pulling the Master along with him. For hours, the big dog churned through the water, his massive paws driving with deep, powerful strokes.

At long last, Trevor struggled onto the beach. Then, with the little strength that remained in his body, he dragged the Master out of the water — and to safety.

The next day, it was raining when Josh finally led Miss Elly and Uncle Leo back to where he had last seen Trevor. Uncle Leo called out loudly, hoping to hear an answer. But the shore was deserted, and the only sound was the rain, pelting down on the sandy beach.

For several days, they continued to search the forest and the shoreline. But the rain had washed away any trace of Trevor or the Master.

Then one day, as the rain was finally letting up, Josh discovered a single paw print, deeply imbedded in the sandy beach. His keen sense of smell told him that it had been left there by Trevor.

"Wow, Oh Bow Wow!" Josh shouted excitedly, to let the others know what he had found.

Soon, Josh located a path which led to a rustic cabin. The little dog raced ahead, then waited anxiously for the others to catch up with him.

Miss Elly nervously patted the little dog's neck, as Uncle Leo knocked on the door. There was the sound of movement from inside the cabin, and the wait seemed endless. Uncle Leo knocked again.

Slowly the door creaked open, and out stepped the Master, with his eyes covered with white bandages. Trevor walked close by the Master's side, almost as if they were joined together.

Josh immediately noticed something grasped tightly in the Master's hand. It was the leash which Trevor had long before learned to fear. But now, the leash was made into a harness and fitted around Trevor's chest.

The little dog looked into Trevor's eyes, expecting to see the fear which had been there not long before. Instead, he saw a look of happiness. "Wow, Oh Bow Wow," Josh whispered.

"Trevor saved my life," said the Master, as he started to cry. And he told them what had happened out on the bay. "My eyes were hurt, and Trevor was able to get help for me. He has been acting as my seeing-eye dog, and seems eager to help me."

"I never understood that someone could be so loving, and yet so brave and strong," sobbed the Master. "He has taught me a valuable lesson. I only hope that he can someday forgive me for the way I treated him."

In time, the Master's eyes healed, and he was able to see again. But he never saw things more clearly than he did that awful day.

The Master talked often with Miss Elly and Uncle Leo, and learned to be a friend to animals. He even offered to help out at Uncle Leo's shelter.

With the Master's help, Trevor wrote to the school for the blind, to find out if he could become a real seeing-eye dog. Trevor had willingly helped during the Master's blindness, because he felt needed and important.

And the Master promised that he would never again try to make Trevor become a hunting dog. For the Master had learned that it is our own dreams which are important, and not the dreams which others would have us follow.

Spring gave way to summer, and summer ended all too soon. It had been an exciting and memorable vacation, one that Josh would not soon forget. But finally, it was time to go home to Bobsled.

As Josh and Trevor said goodbye, they knew that they would always be friends, even though they lived far apart.

And the Master became allergic to Trevor. Now, whenever he hugs the big, brown dog, he breaks out — in a great, big smile.

It was the doggonest vacation ever.